About the Author

Polly was born and grew up in Cornwall, situated in a little village on the north coast. Her dreams became a reality when she got in to theatre school and onto circus school in Bristol where the magic began and she travelled with one of the best trapeze artists currently in the UK. Life has been rich and beautiful as opportunities opened up in her life. Three wonderful daughters later, Polly returned to the little village of her past and bought her family house, which has cradled her as she finished writing up this book before starting chemo and fighting for her life. The focus of her girls' future and the divine got her through. 'It's been a journey,' says Polly, 'I wrote this book in 2012. I believe life is all about timing. Now is the time for Princess Podockee. I give thanks every day for all I have learnt. For life is one big lesson and not a rehearsal. If you don't stop once in a while and breathe in the beauty and magic of life, you could miss it. I walk forwards with an open wild heart full of love and excitement at the next chapters of my own story. May you all travel in your own truth, for you alone know your own rhythm. I hope you enjoy this book as much as I did writing it.
Peace out.
Polly Xx'

Dedications

To the best Pa in the world…who never gave up on that little girl.

To Mum Mags, thank you for always believing in my light and being a light when my own was not shining.

To my brother, who I have missed more than spent time with but who has always had my heart. Thank you for your inspiration.

To the most amazing, beautiful and pure daughters a mother could ever, ever ask for…Lila, Honeymalou and Marnie, you kept me alive.

To Moss, the children we have made are a thousand birthdays and Christmases rolled into three beautiful gifts. A treasure beyond measure. Thank you for being you.

To the friends who have my back…your love is a gift and I love to share it with you all.

P. W. Doodle

PRINCESS PODOCKEE AND THE LAND OF TING

Illustrated by James Marchant

AUSTIN MACAULEY PUBLISHERS™

LONDON • CAMBRIDGE • NEW YORK • SHARJAH

A CIP catalogue record for this title is available from the British Library.

ISBN 9781398408265 (Paperback)
ISBN 9781398414358 (ePub e-book)

www.austinmacauley.com

First Published (2021)
Austin Macauley Publishers Ltd
25 Canada Square
Canary Wharf
London
E14 5LQ

Acknowledgements

To Austin Macauley for putting my story into print. Vinh, thank you for answering many questions.

To my talented brother, I am your biggest fan! Your drawings and artwork blow me away. Thank you for saying yes and coming on this journey with me…forever your skin and blister. X

To myself for struggling on with the one fingered type, until I got faster and didn't give up!
For keeping my head up and light bright as I walked through the darkness.

To my consultant Adam Forbes for listening and knowing when to stop, your team in haematology are stars.

To my family and friends, you are my life blood!

Contents

IN THE BEGINNING 11

DRAGONS ARE FRIENDS 18

TRAVEL WITH LIGHT 24

THIS ISN'T GOODBYE 27

THE JOURNEY BEGINS 32

WE LIKE A PLAN 35

BRINGING BACK THE BALANCE 37

FOLLOWING HER CALLING 40

FOCUS 43

RACE AGAINST TIME 47

HOME 49

IN THE BEGINNING

Once upon a time in a land much further than Penzance, even past the Isle of Scilly, there lived a very brave, a very colourful and a very special princess. The special comes from Princess Podockee never growing old and never being young. She just is and always has been. She just remembers waking up one day and there she was on Ting. She has had no mother to hold her and no father to read her softly to sleep as you or I have had.

Princess Podockee is not as you would imagine a 'normal' princess to be...Oh, you know, the ones that live in castles or the ones that await in a sleeping slumber for their long-lost Prince to arrive...Or the ones that are just born into a life most of us could never comprehend. No no, our princess is the real deal. She believes in unity and one love. Princess Podockee understands the great gift that we are all part of each other in the great circle of life. As well as being very colourful and brave.

Now Ting...wonderful Ting is an island with many interesting inhabitants, from wise old dragons to four-legged friends big, small, tiny, finned, feathered and forked, to the knowledgeable island folk. Ting itself is very hard to find on our modern-day maps because one of the most amazing things about Ting is that it moves. Every season, the fishes that surround Ting make the great journey to the bottom of the ocean, where they begin to detach the millions of sea anemones with their super sucks and move the island. The inhabitants of Ting do not know where they will be taken each season but without fail, every season, Ting changes position as sure as the sumptuous summer turns into autumn.

One important thing that the inhabitants of Ting know is that they ALL have to be present when Ting moves or they will be lost forever on an ever changing tide. Fear not, this has not happened as of yet and so our true story begins one gloriously sunny day on Ting.

It was summer and the dazzling sun was high in the sky shooting out jets of sparkles to the ocean, which joyously twinkled and rippled back in return. On this fine morning, Princess Podockee was woken very abruptly by one of her winged guard dogs, howling at the bottom of her grand treehouse. She rolled out of her bunk, landing with a thud on her sheepskin rugs (which brought instant comfort to her out-of-bed toes as they sank into its woolly depths). Her eyes were all a blur and hair all skewwhiff. She looked around for her tutu.

As she rubbed her ocean eyes, her vision became focused and she saw it lying only yards away on the wooden floorboards. She pulled it on, the colourful mass of netting and lace darting in all directions. Princess Podockee wolfed down some bircher muesli and proceeded to her rather cool basket lift. As she entered the lift, she untied the fastened ropes at the top. She let them go smoothly through her palms until they pulled tight and she began to sail down to the bottom with great speed.

"Wooooooo hooooo! What a wake-up ride," Princess Podockee sang as she sailed down. By the time she was on the ground, her winged guard dog Che Free had flown to greet her, his tongue out sideways and his eyes all spritely.

"Ruff snuff...Good morning to you, Podockee."

"Hello, dear Che Free, where are the others?"

"Ruff snuff...Sleeping in the branches of your tree!"

Princess Podockee spun on one heel, looked and laughed. "Hhhaaaahhoooooha, so they are. Why were you howling, dear boy?"

Che Free took a deep breath. "The wind of change, I smelt them coming in on the soft breezes from the ocean."

Princess Podockee pondered. "Well, Che Free, the fishes will be making their deep sea descent over the coming days and Ting will move. Is it not that?"

"Uuummmmm ruff. No, Podockee, another smell. In fact, all the animals are talking about it, from the smallest to the wisest old dragons."

"Well," she said, stretching into a yogic warrior position, "I will take a swim and see if I can feel it; take word to the colourful Gomowwa dragon, I will be there soon."

"Ruff ruff teehoo, Podockee," and with that he soared into the sky, his yellow fur gleaming in the sunlight.

Princess Podockee began to run. She ran through the trees. "Morning!" she yelled. Cartwheeling through the poppiest field you have ever seen. "Good day, poppies," she sang, up and over the sand dunes, still running until she had reached the top of the last dune. She perched up there and caught her breath, the vast blue ocean laid out before her, its blue wonder always mesmerising her. "Good morning, Mum," she called to the ocean smiling, before crouching down and starting to slide down the last sand dune with one foot forwards to the bottom. She looked like she was riding a wave, a huge sand wave; the wind blew through her hair as she picked up speed to the bottom. She walked to the seashore and with weary legs, she welcomed the water as the first waves broke over her feet...her toes tingled as she waded in.

When she was deep enough, she dived in, immersing her whole body into the cool, salty, satisfying water. Diving to the bottom, Princess Podockee reached out and grabbed a handful of sand then, somersaulting around, pushed off the sea bed to the surface. As she broke through the water and her body rose out, she flicked her hair back and drew in a deep breath.

"Paaaaah," she sucked in the fresh air around her as the droplets of water danced mid-air before gravity took them down, splashing everywhere.

"Thank you!" she shouted, her voice echoing around. "Thank you for this morning and everything in my life."

She swam back to the shore, tutu still intact and steadily walked out of the waves to the sand where she began to shake herself dry, like a wet dog. A good thorough shake, her cheeks wobbling, her hair fanning out, spraying water everywhere.

After her momentary manic movement was over, she stood tall and took in long deep breaths. Princess Podockee crouched down and placed both palms on the sand, closing her eyes she listened. All she could hear at first was the ocean lapping on the shore. She cleared her thoughts and listened with a silent mind, pushing her hands deeper into the sand. She felt a light heartbeat, a low trembling almost like...like...she pushed her hands deeper still...like something millions of miles away was hurting, something connected with the earth itself...Something big. Podockee stood up, lost in thought as she walked to the shore to rinse her hands off. She looked once again at the horizon and felt words come into her heart.

"I feel you and I will help you."

Princess Podockee lifted her hands into a prayer position and bowed her head to the ocean. "Catcha soon, Mum," she whispered, smiling through her fingertips. She turned on her heel with a spring in her step and headed off to Gomowwa's dwelling.

DRAGONS ARE FRIENDS

It was mid-morning by the time she reached the forgotten woods and walked into the clearing, where the Princess's eyes lit up as she saw the magnificent structure of Gomowwa Garwinkle. The dragon was watching the ocean and inhaling and exhaling buckets of salty air. The island's coastline was much wilder over this side and a lot more rugged.

"Hellooooo, darling Gomowwa," Princess Podockee sang on her approach.

Gomowwa turned her elegant head slowly. "Rrrrrr, mmmyyyy dddear Podockeeeeee, welcome! It has been some time since our paths last crossed, I have miiiiist youuu."

As they reached each other, Gomowwa lowered her great head to the Princess.

"Me too," Podockee replied, flinging her arms around the leathery dragon's neck. She gripped tightly and nuzzled her face deep into her neck.

"Uuummmm," Gomowwa smiled as they embraced. "Now then, mmyyy dearrr, are you hungry? I have dragonfruit, a drac na loaf in the clay oven and of course, some of myyyy golden elixir bubbling on the stove."

Princess Podockee beamed. "Ooooooo, you read my mind, will you ever tell me the secret to your golden elixir?"

Gomowwa pondered. "Ummm, well, I can tell you the main ingredient."

Podockee's eyes flashed. "Yes...Yes."

Gomowwa smiled. "Ummm, why, that's LOVE; I put it in all my makings."

As she said this, the beautiful dragon opened her mouth and let out a puff of smoke, which formed a tremendous heart shape, and she winked. The friends began to giggle. "Hhhaaahh heeee oh hooo."

"Come come," Gomowwa said, catching her breath. "Siiiiit down, Podockee."

Podockee hopped into a nearby hammock as Gomowwa headed off to the clay oven. The hammock nearly swallowed Podockee up with its size. Gomowwa heard yelps and giggles as she turned around to see a sprawl of legs and arms, then finally Princess Podockee's head popping up.

"Hahahahaha, dear friend, I must make you another, a smaller one to suit."

"Hehehehe no, no, it's half the fun. No worries."

The great dragon turned and pulled out a steaming, sweet smelling drac na loaf from the clay oven.

"Ummm, my puffiest yet."

Princess Podockee's eyes took in the loaf. "Dear friend, you have excelled yourself."

She sniffed up gushes of steaming drac na loaf.

"Oooooo."

Gomowwa glided here and glided there and soon there was a steaming plate of gorgeous foods and at the centre of the table, as promised, was the golden elixir, sitting proudly, bubbling away with two handmade clay goblets next to it. (She had even made a miniature one for Podockee.) When the dragon had finally sat down, the friends both smiled at one another and gave thanks for the great company and delightful feast they were both about to devour.

All went silent as they picked, drank, burped, pardon me'd, ummed and yummed a lot. They sat back, satisfied, with their eyes closed.

Gomowwa was the first to break the silence.

"Ummm, Che Free arrived early this morning with a message of your arrival and of his worriessss of this 'change'."

Princess Podockee sat up alert. "Yes, he started howling as soon as he smelt it, nearly waking up the whole tree. I myself knelt down by the shore this morning and felt a low tremor; it felt like something many miles away is hurting and needs our help...But—"

"Ahhh," Gomowwa interrupted. "It does need our help. It is a large creature that has been coming into my dreams."

"But, but what can we do and how can we help it. Soon the fishes of Ting will be making their deep sea descent and all the members of Ting have to be present. Or we will be lost out there forever."

Princess Podockee gazed out at the endless ocean.

Gomowwa looked lovingly at Podockee. "It is our destiny to help this creature, for the life of the whole ocean depends on the survival of it; without the ocean, we are all doomed."

Princess Podockee looked startled at her friend's words. "How, how does the ocean survive by this creature? The ocean is vast and abundant and ever alive as you or I...no one is running us?"

Gomowwa took a deep breath. "Ummm, we are all part of a great energy and part of that energy lives in this creature! As you said, dear friend, Ting will move with or without us. Time is not on our side."

"Do you have a plan, darling Gomowwa?"

"Yessss, but we cannot do it alone. Summon your winged guard dogs; we must take only the fittest. I will gather the dragons, we set off at dusk!"

"Dusk!" Princess Podockee was surprised. "So so soon."

"The time is nigh, dearest Podockee."

With that, the mighty dragon rose up, leaving Podockee struggling out of her hammock. Gomowwa wrapped up some drac na loaf for the princess's journey back to her treehouse. They looked at each other knowingly and nodded. This quest was going to need a lot of bravery, courage and strength. They smiled and set off on their separate ways. As Podockee faded into the distance, she heard Gomowwa's voice on the wind.

"We leave from Tallakoo bay."

TRAVEL WITH LIGHT

Princess Podockee moved with great haste along the coast, up and down the sun-soaked dunes, through the poppiest meadow you have ever seen, up and on through the woods, still stomping until she had arrived at the clearing of her own wonderful treehouse. There, she stopped and took some moments to take in the homely heartfelt view in front of her. How she would miss this—the old gnarled roots of the tree with clumps of moss dotted perfectly in-between them. The strong, tall tree trunk of the old oak that held up her masterpiece home. Her mind drifted to her comfy bed and all the luxuries Ting offered. Leaving it with the uncertainty of her return was terrifying, a little bit of her heart would be left behind, she shook her head.

"No, no," she said to herself, "it's time to give back, a Princess ain't a Princess for nothing, maybe I will find out more about myself. I have never left my beloved Ting before."

With a stronger head, she walked over to a colourful wooden box that sat happily on tall sturdy legs. It was a music box; she turned the long golden handle and the box opened, music started to chime out of it, quietly at first then louder and louder until sweet-sounding melodies were pouring out of the quaint box, echoing around her treehouse clearing and soaking into the trees. Princess Podockee was summoning her winged guard dogs; as the music drifted higher and higher on the wind, a mass of yellow fur and wings came flying through the sky, some came in fluttering, some soaring and some dive-bombing down.

As soon as their paws touched the ground, they all began grooving to the musical beats. They danced in a large circle around Podockee (who laughed and laughed for her own legs couldn't stop dancing either).

She carefully closed the lid and the music ended. With her guard dogs focused on her and their wings crossed neatly behind their backs, she began to tell them all about the quest that awaited them.

"Some of you I need to stay here and keep guard of Ting, it will be down to you to keep the creatures and island folk safe, if Ting does move without us...(as she said this, she glanced down and her shoulders slumped a little) Ting will need all the help it can get."

"We would follow you to the end of the earth, Podockee." They all howled in agreement.

"Ooh! Thank you, thank you, dear hearts, my loyal guard dogs, I love you all, we will be faced with the unknown, your strength and loyalty makes me even stronger. Thank you." She walked around them stroking their elegant heads.

"I shall only take four of you, Che Free, Jara, Bamboo and Bear! We must assemble the necessary provisions...we must travel light. Meet me at the shoreline at dusk."

The four saluted with a glint in their eyes and flew off. "The rest of you...I need you to be my eyes and ears when I am gone, please go and tell the inhabitants of Ting what is going on." They too saluted and darted off in different directions.

THIS ISN'T GOODBYE

Princess Podockee walked towards her basket lift, got in and began pulling the ropes up to her treehouse. She tied off the rope at the top and climbed out. Opening her door, the smells and sights of her humble abode brought warmth and comfort to her body. Jumping up onto her bunk, she dived face-first into her pillow.

"I am going to miss you," she muffled into it. Slowly prising herself from her precious pillow, she reached behind it and pulled out her lucky leaf. (Podockee had carved it out of a chunk of oak from her very own tree, when the winter's storms had taken their toll and a branch had been struck down.) Opening the leather pouch around her waist, she popped it in, tapping it for safety. Climbing down from her bunk, she took one last look around her treehouse as the afternoon sun streamed in from the windows.

"I will come back you know, just try and stop me." Winking and smiling at the empty room, she closed the door.

Gomowwa was at the ready with three statuesque dragons. Most of the other dragons were too old to adventure any more, their wings had been hung up long ago with only their stories left to live on. But what stories they were.(These are most definitely stories for you to hear another time.) But for now, the wise ones had sent forth Gomowwa with luck dust and energy bubbles to be used ONLY in times of need.

News had already spread around the island. Animals and island folk had all begun to gather at Tallakoo bay to wave off the adventurers. Princess Podockee was striding up the last dune with fire in her belly as she reached the top. Standing strong on top of the dune, the wind blowing through her hair and tutu. She looked down upon the bay. There, before her, was a sight to behold — all the inhabitants of Ting had gathered...never before had the princess seen every member present like this. Thoughts filled Podockee's head.

"United we stand, dear friends, seeing this gives me even more courage and determination to save this animal and get back in time before Ting moves." She looked to her left, casting her eyes upon her beloved winged guard dogs. Surrounding them were animals of every kind. In the middle of the bay stood four colourful grand dragons (Gomowwa was the smallest, if you could call her small); at the foot of the dune, awaiting Princess Podockee were the colourful island folk. A bolt of excitement shot up through her body as she began to take big moon steps down to the bottom, she smiled with arms open as the islanders began to greet her with petals. They had even laid a path of bracken for her to walk down.

As Podockee walked along, she thanked every member. Some gave her blessings for the adventure ahead and others just wanted to squeeze her hand in support. Again, she thanked them and headed towards the central group. The dragons and winged guard dogs were waiting for her, quite bewildered because a large circle had congregated around them all. The circle was made up of island folk and animals all singing and dancing a ritual dance of safety and luck. Haunting tribal noises echoed around the island as their tempo built. Podockee couldn't help but give a loving giggle at her companions' faces as she entered the circle.

The dancers raised their arms up to the sky, moving faster and faster around until...zoooom...they all fell to the ground and all went silent. The dragons were the first ones to let out a "Raaaaaawwww" of appreciation, followed by the winged guard dogs barking and howling and Princess Podockee manically clapping shouting, "Thank you. Thank you...we take your energy and love with us."

Podockee walked over to Gomowwa and stroked her ridged back.

"It's time, dear friend."

As dusk fell all around them, Podockee climbed upon Gomowwa's back.

"Islanders of Ting, we will be back, your united love travels forwards with us, keep your hearts positive and alert, we shall return."

As she finished her last line, Gomowwa had begun to open her wings.

"Now we fly."

The travellers began to rise from the sandy bay as the last sun beams shot across the ocean. The islanders watched in awe as the brave adventurers became silhouetted against a maroon sky.

THE JOURNEY BEGINS

They travelled for the first few miles in silence, Princess Podockee hugged tightly around Gomowwa's neck.

"My dear friend, we have a loong journey ahead of us, before we make the dive into the ocean, we shall all rest. But now, my friend, sleeep."

"Yes," yawned Podockee, and she snuggled down into Gomowwa's neck, her eyelids becoming heavier and heavier as the wind hummed around them.

When Princess Podockee woke up, she found herself covered in blankets. She peeled back the fluffy covers only to see a world of white. Standing up, the white world was bright and fluffy...white, bright and fluffy?

"Clouds...But how can I be standing on clouds? Where are we?"

"You're awake then?"

Podockee turned to see where the voice was coming from, the others were in a circle a few yards away. She stumbled forwards and as she straightened up, Podockee realised she was hovering...just above the clouds. Walking a little uneasily to her companions, she joined the circle. Che Free looked at his princess.

"Ruff snuff, you have been sleeping for some time, we have covered many miles, Podockee."

"That's good news, hhaa sorry I slept so long, if I had strong wings I would carry you all." Princess Podockee lifted her arms and made slow winged movements, the group chuckled.

"Your energy will be needed before the end," Gomowwa smiled.

"Are we in the clouds?" Podockee said as she looked around.

"Yes," called Bamboo.

"Wow! I have never been in the clouds before, it's so beautiful up here, all white and peaceful, it's like...like...heaven, well, what I imagine heaven to be like. You know, I didn't realise you can sit in the clouds." Princess Podockee grinned.

The dragons let out rawwwing laughter. "You can't," Gomowwa smiled. "I have sssssprinked luck dust upon us all. This is why you are ever so slightly hovering just above them."

Podockee looked around the circle. "Yes, oh yes, hheeaaa."

WE LIKE A PLAN

Che Free got up on his paws. "Podockee, when we get to the right spot in the ocean, we will fly up directly above it and have our final meeting in the clouds. Only three of us will make the dive down to the bottom of the ocean—myself, Gomowwa and you, dear Princess. The others will be our protectors above and will listen, hidden in the safety of the clouds."

Gomowwa was the next to speak, "Theeee wise old dragons who have had many adventures long before usssss have given me energy bubbles. These energy bubbles act like a second skin and will enable us to breath under water for long periods of timmmme."

Princess Podockee put her hand up, the group smiled.

"Can we use our hands with the bubbles around us? You know, so we can help the creature?"

"Yesss," replied Gomowwa, "and they will protect us at the same time."

"Fantastic." Podockee's mind drifted back to the work ahead. "What will we find when we are down there, is the creature friendly, why is it in trouble?"

Gomowwa took a deep breath. "My dreams seem to tell me it knows we are coming, for we are all connected. The creature is covered by man's pollution, for years it has swallowed all the rubbish and waste that the human race have dumped in the water. Over the last few years, man has become careless and dumped even more. The creature has no energy to tackle the toxins. Without this creature turning the waste into coral and giving new life and habitats to the sea world, all will be lost.

"We won't be alone; the giant underwater mammals will be there to join us. Only together do we have a chance to change this."

Princess Podockee looked alarmed. "How can we stop man from doing this in the future?"

"The big waves have already hit most of the world's coastlines, the creature has tried to spit this pollution out, the force has created big waves of rubble and rubbish. Man came to the shore and made a deal with the ocean. If the waves stopped and their children and families were saved, they would teach their children and their children's children to respect Mother Ocean; They promised to only use what they needed and to use natural materials once again. Plastic is killing everything. The times are changing, deaaarr Princess, man will once again be connected with their earth."

"Oh geeee whizz...by golly! It's about time, I am ready to help in any way I can!"

Podockee was as much nervous and excited to be a part of this historic change. Well rested, her companions got up and readied themselves to take flight, Podockee mounted Gomowwa, thoughts of her beloved Ting and splendid life flashed through her mind's eye, but she focused all her energy on the task awaiting them.

BRINGING BACK THE BALANCE

They soared out of the clouds, hitting big gushes of sea breezes and spray. Gomowwa flew down just above the waves, the sea was so ferocious, with no land in sight they flew on and on. After miles, Podockee felt the pace slow and the group flew up to gather in the clouds.

When they had caught their breath, Gomowwa parted some of the cloud with her claws. "Arrr yesss, this is the spot, looook." The others all looked in turn; when it was Podockee's turn, she gazed down through the white tunnel. As it had been moments before, the ferocious sea raged on but directly underneath them was an area of complete stillness. It was about the size of a small lake. The water seemed totally unaffected by the rest of the ocean's movements.

"Haaaaaaa, talk about X marks the spot," Podockee exclaimed. Che Free puffed out his chest. "Ruff ruff, do you have the energy bubbles...now is the time."

Gomowwa nodded her elegant head and pulled out three glimmering liquid gold bags. She threw one of the jelly-like liquids over the princess and as soon as it touched the top of her head, it rushed down her body, engulfing her like it was her own skin. She placed one upon her own head and passed one to Che Free. They all glowed and sparkled.

Che Free saluted to the others and made his dive down through the cloud tunnel —shhhhhhhh spaaaalosh. Gomowwa turned to the others and spoke with a glint in her eye...that if trouble DID occur, she would send sparks out of the ocean.

Out of that very spot Che Free had just dived into. She looked down and took a deep breath, readying herself to dive.

"Wait," one of her dragons roared, grabbing her arm. "What happens if your signal can't get to us and something happens to you down there?"

Gomowwa smiled. "I will follow you in my mind; we shall be each other's eyes below and above." The great dragons locked heads and passed energy between one another. "I will be there for you, dear friend." Gomowwa winked and smiled then turned and dived out of the clouds—shhhhhh swoooooshhhh. The sea surged up in her wake. Princess Podockee was next; she hugged all of her remaining guard dogs.

"Good luck, our Princess," they barked in chorus. She turned and gracefully dived out of the clouds—shhhhhh plop.

FOLLOWING HER CALLING

As the princess entered the water, the world around her became dark and quiet. She did not feel the normal cool tingly sensation when one usually enters the ocean; the energy bubble puffed out a little and created a warm flexible layer. As her eyes adjusted, she began to see huge shadows swimming towards a fixed point...down down to the bottom of the ocean bed. Two glowing bubbles came into view, radiant against the deep blue surroundings. Gomowwa signalled to them to follow her and she led the way.

A school of white fish finned past them, followed by a jeeegumbus whale, the white fish swimming next to this great mammal highlighted the old barnacles on its body as they hurried past. As the whale's great eye passed Gomowwa, it winked, its tail slowly undulating as it cruised at its own speed downwards. More and more fish folk appeared as they swam on, Princess Podockee realised they were swimming into some sort of a tunnel and it was starting to get lighter as they swam on, soulful singing started to enrich the water. Podockee's heart started to fill with empathy and sorrow as she tuned into this creature's sound, it was calling her...it was hurting. The power of the creature's energy over-whelmed her but she kept focused and swam on, intrigued at what they would find.

The tunnel opened out into a clearing and as the princess's eyes became more settled and focused on her new surroundings, she saw before them a hive of activity. Rubbish, rubbish everywhere of every kind was tangled, knotted and piled high.

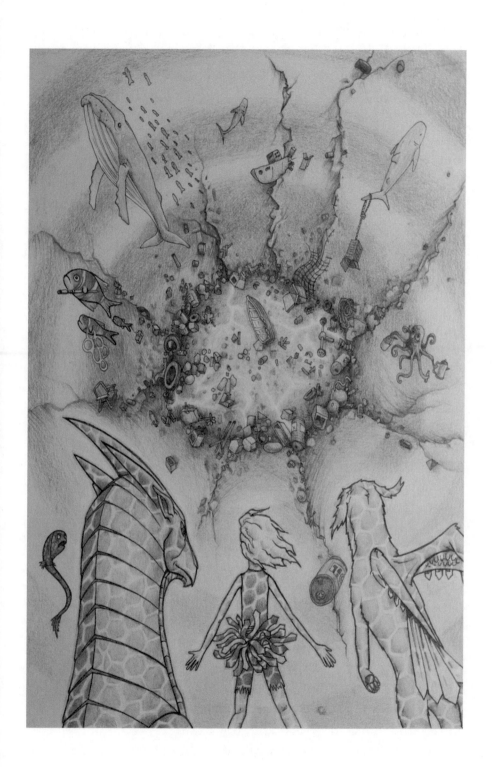

The smaller fish were darting back and forth carrying small lumps in their fins and around their necks. Some were even working as a team to move larger mounds. In the middle was the magnificent whale beating off clumps of rotten rubbish with its tail. Sea folk of every species would then pull, separate, dig and load the masses of rubbish and take it to the side before hurrying back for another load.

How long have they been doing this, Podockee thought, if only man could see the devastation rubbish causes. The creature's song now filled the space around...yet there was no sign of the creature itself. Podockee, Gomowwa and Che Free came into a circle and held hands. As they connected to each other, they began to read each other's thoughts. Gomowwa's voice sounded first. "The fiisssh and mammals are moving a lot but we need to heal this creature from the inside."

Che Free piped up, "Ruff ruff, if we head straight for the middle, we will have a better chance at reaching it. I shall lead and use my wings and claws to break through."

"Iiii also," Gomowwa said. "What about me?" Princess Podockee sighed.

"My deeearrr princesss, we will need you before the end more than you will ever know. Keep close to us and stay alert and focused. You will know when you are needed." They felt a gush of love surge between them as they broke the circle and Gomowwa and Che Free led on.

They both charged straight in, attacking the pollution with full force. Podockee sent a little prayer up of protection and thanks for the energy bubbles, which were like steel as the rubbish flew this way and that, bouncing off their glittering bubbles as it hit. Their hard work was soon paying off as they tunnelled deeper into the rubbish, which had become an undulating mass of brown goo, thick and dense. Still, the great dragon ploughed on and in with determination and power.

FOCUS

The creature's song had become so loud now that Podockee could think of nothing else as it consumed her every thought. Che Free stopped and pawed at Princess Podockee, Gomowwa halted and gently picked up Podockee's hand and placed it on a solid mass. It felt warm to touch...it was breathing...they had made contact with the creature. Che Free scraped around Podockee's hand and in the gloom, the light from their energy bubbles made out a nose. Podockee knew what to do and they cleared the creature's airways. The creature's song dwindled as it began to suck up and out deep breaths.

Gomowwa hoisted the Princess up onto the giant's nose and Podockee straddled it as if she had mounted a horse. Placing both of her hands firmly onto the enormous nose, Podockee started to send energy into it. Gomowwa and Che Free began to clear the goo from around its mouth, other sea life had entered the tunnel they had made and were breaking up the rubble in their wake.

Podockee felt a tingling surge of power come over her as she filled the creature with pure love and light...her hands were hot as the energies raced like fireworks out of her. As she fell into a trance, the creature's song became louder and louder, not the sorrowful heartache that had sounded before but a beautiful song, a song filled with magic and hope...so powerful were its chants that the whole ocean became intoxicated with it, louder and louder. Princess Podockee didn't move a muscle as the noise stopped and the world around became silent. Like the ocean itself was holding its breath...then BAAAAAAAAAAA BOOOOOSSHHHH! The black-brown goo surrounding the creature burst into a million tiny pieces. Shhhhhhhhwwaaaaaaap. Everything and everybody was frozen, a moment in time where you are powerless to our greater life force, the universal energy that connects us all.

As the ocean took a breath again and life carried on, Princess Podockee, Che Free, Gomowwa and all the other animals fell motionless onto the sea bed, the teeny tiny specks landing all around them. Everything was quiet and still. Above them rested an almighty creature, full of energy, sparkles darting out of its eyes. It had huge long seaweed hair, unravelling down like the mane of a lion. Its gigantic body was made up of the most colourful coral, limpets, barnacles, muscles, pebbles and sand, all undulating as it breathed in deep breaths. An electric magnificent monster made up of the ocean itself. It looked down at the motionless beings below. He sang his name, Ooooommmbaa. Omba was free, sparks still flying from his eyes as he cast them upon the settled scene below, twinkling beneath the dust. Omba could see the energy bubbles, focusing on Podockee, he raised her up with his eyes, limp and fragile was her small body. He lifted her up in front of his eyes and she began to slowly spin...her energy bubble changing from rich pink to purple and finally white light.

Podockee started to wake up...she stretched as if waking up from the most peaceful dream. Only to find herself eye to eye with the most powerful creature she had ever encountered. Omba's eyes glowed as he looked into Podockee's. Rich with every shade of blue and green you can think of, with electric yellows darting through the middle. Coral made up his eyelashes.

Princess Podockee spoke in her mind...*it's you...it's...you are the reason for our journey.* A soothing voice entered her head, "I am Omba...I thank you...I thank you all. Your work is done, the oceans are saved." Princess Podockee felt excitement shoot through her.

Omba spoke again, "I leave you with these words...your future is bright, enjoy every moment and be present in each day, you have the gift of knowing you are never alone, for the very flowers are your friends. Spread your light to others, show them the way to truth and beauty but remember to keep enough for yourself."

Princess Podockee listened intently then her mind snapped back to the present moment. "My, my friends..." She looked around and she saw the figures beneath her. "Oh noooo!" Fear flew into her. "Please please, let them be okay." Her heart started to ache. "Please Omba, help me wake them...to help all the creatures here that helped you."

She stared into his eyes...and a smooth voice sounded in her head again, "Do not let fear take over...focus." She felt a jumble of emotions then she quietened her mind and looked back into his eyes and spoke calmly, "The love that flows through me is strong enough to bring life back into them."

"Yesssssss," the smooth voice echoed. "They are weak...we must breathe energy into them."

Podockee turned and swam towards her friends; the great Omba lowered his head. The motionless figures began to glow with the same colours Princess Podockee had, she hovered motionless next to the great figure as he worked his magic, Podockee began to focus on her friends' hearts and sent them both a huge amount of pure love.

One by one they opened their eyes...she rushed towards them, reaching out for a paw and claw. Once they were together, a new energy field surrounded them all and they slowly started to float up. Podockee held tight to her friends as she looked down at the ocean floor below; two outstanding eyes were looking back up at her...she thanked Omba with her eyes and promised she would always share her light. As the new energy field touched the surface, sparks began to spurt out, jets of turquoise, pink, purple and gold. Giant wings came soaring through the colours, weaving in and out of them were Podockee's loyal guard dogs.

Once again the team was united and they cradled their weary friends in their paws and claws...beating their wings furiously against the ocean's waves. Princess Podockee let out a big breath of relief as her body relaxed and she fell into a deep slumber.

RACE AGAINST TIME

When she awoke, she could hear the mighty wings above her undulating as the wind whistled through them. She was encased in ferocious-looking claws but they held her so delicately, not squashing a limb. Podockee stretched and began to peek through; to her left was Che Free lying motionless in more cradling claws and to her right was Gomowwa's stiff body being carried through the sky, she looked like a plank of wood. A very heavy plank of wood at that. She rolled on her back and looked up; Podockee could make out a few of the winged guard dogs.

As the world around them sped on, they were all in silence. Princess Podockee thought over their adventure, she sent out a prayer to mankind. "I wish for you all to be mindful of our Mother Earth, of each other and the energy that connects us all. From this energy, we are all made of...from this energy we shall all return."

The wind blew on as they raced through the clouds, the scales of the great dragons shimmered as the evening sun hit them. Evening...alarm bells sounded in Podockee's head...Ting, her beloved Ting. How long had they been down at the bottom of the ocean? Ting was due to move and if it had moved before they got back, they would be lost forever. She tried to clear her worrying mind, replacing it with a positive light visualisation of everything being complete.

HOME

She looked to the horizon, bubbles of excitement landed in her tummy. Could it be, could it really be...Podockee rubbed her eyes for a clearer look through the great claws. She held her breath, searching madly...butteries flew into her tummy, darting about everywhere. "Ting, ohhh, it's Ting." She could just make out the island's unique shape silhouetted against the setting sun, it was a rich sunset. "We are home," she whispered with soft satisfying lips. "Home."

The sky darted with golds, auburn reds, oranges and as the deep purples seeped into the mix, the velvet curtains of night were drawn to a close. Princess Podockee could feel them descending, as the ground got closer, Podockee realised they were on the other side of the island to her treehouse, down at the most easterly corner of Ting, home of the witch doctor. The great dragons beat their wings steadily and with the utmost care placed our three heroes on the soft earth. They soared up high then landed elegantly to the side of them, the winged guard dogs had flown ahead to collect the others from the Princess's tree and were now all flying in...black silky shadows against a carpet of dazzling stars.

Princess Podockee got up stiffly and walked over to Che Free, her winged guard dogs made a circle around them both, arranging their wings and crossing them neatly behind their back as they looked upon their motionless master. Princess Podockee knelt down next to Che Free and placed one palm flat against his heart and the other hand rested upon his head. She closed her eyes, warmth rushed through her body and tingled down her arms and out through her fingertips. Che

Free's body began to glow, the winged guard dogs tightened their circle as their master opened his eyes. He looked at Podockee. "Ruff rrrr grrrrrr, thank you."

"Sssshhh," she replied soothingly, "rest, dear friend, rest." She left the winged guards dogs surrounding him and strode over to Gomowwa, she had been badly injured from the blast.

A rattling sound filled the night, Podockee turned to see glimpses of fire coming through the trees, it was the island's fireflies. Leading them was the witch doctor; he was a beautifully handsome dark-skinned man with the most delicate bone structure surrounded with white flowing dreadlocks and an array of white feathers, which hung down like a mane to his shoulders. His eyes gleamed and sparkled against the fireflies' light. "Welcome home, sister, you is a healing ting now, me proud! I have come to help you heal Gomowwa."

Princess Podockee got up and flung her arms around him. "Thank you."

They both knelt down. Podockee sat at Gomowwa's heart, crossed her legs and put both palms flat against her chest. The witch doctor settled at her head. The sky spun into a flurry of millions of darting fireflies; soon they settled and formed a perfect circle of glowing energy around the dragon. It seemed now that the whole of Ting was awake and present. They formed four groups around the fireflies' circle, representing north, east, south and west. Together, they began a very low hhhhummmm. On the outside of the islanders sat the statuesque dragons of the island, their eyes were full of energy as they focused their minds and stared upon Gomowwa.

All was still but the lapping of the waves as they broke softly onto Ting's shores. Gomowwa's great jaw opened. "Ummmm, can anyone smell drac na loaf?" Her eyes opened and she winked at the witch doctor. The fireflies broke their circle and rose high into the sky.

Ting itself seemed to breathe out and the inhabitants let out giggles and cheers of relief and happiness. Gomowwa looked down at Podockee. "Deeaarrr friend, we have done it and we are home." Podockee dived onto the dragon's body and held tight. "Until the next adventure, my friend, hhaaaa." Gomowwa breathed out, "Life is innnndeed the greatest adventure and now you know your gift, uuuuse it well."

Princess Podockee pushed her arms up and looked into her friend's eyes. "Thank you for believing in me." She stood up and held her arms open to Ting and bellowed from her belly, "I love you all."

THE END